Thomas Walter Perry

Little Rossie

Thomas Walter Perry

Little Rossie

ISBN/EAN: 9783337714789

Printed in Europe, USA, Canada, Australia, Japan

Cover: Foto ©Andreas Hilbeck / pixelio.de

More available books at **www.hansebooks.com**

LITTLE ROSSIE.

ROVED

Mass. S Society,

To Boys

WHO WANT TO DO RIGHT, BUT FIND IT IS NOT EASY,

THIS

STRICTLY TRUE

ACCOUNT OF A BOY WHO SUFFERED MUCH, BUT LEARNED BY
SUFFERING,

IS

Affectionately dedicated by their friends,

THE AUTHORS.

CONTENTS.

LITTLE ROSSIE.

I.

OUR LITTLE BOY.

"Thou enviable being,
No storms, no clouds in thy blue sky foreseeing."

OUR little boy was a rogue; I do not mean that he meant to be troublesome to anybody, for he loved all his friends very much, and would have been very sorry if they had not loved him; but he was one of those active little fellows that manage to accomplish a great deal in a day; and, of course, he wanted to do many things that did not specially belong to him, and which he could not do at all well.

If he did a deal of mischief, no one could help loving him, he was so bright and sweet about it all, and had so many queer old speeches to make to account for it.

Our little boy was pretty, too; he had bright auburn hair and brown eyes, and people petted him so much that he would have been spoiled if his father and mother had not been careful of him, for he liked his own way very much, and felt quite sure that what he wanted to do was the best thing.

But I have not told his name, though it was always to be heard over the house, whether little "Rossie" was running about his own home or his grandfather's, at which he spent a great deal of his

time ; for he was so fortunate as to have
two homes where he was loved and
cared for, and to be able to go very easily from one to the other. His grandparents lived in the next town, and were
always glad to have Rossie and his little
brother come to them. The children's
house was not specially interesting; it
stood in a crowded factory village on the
Quinnebaug, where they had no grounds
to play in, nor any woods in which they
could climb about; so it was like going to
paradise for the little fellows to be welcomed to the large garden, where they
were at liberty to climb. the great old
trees for ripe fruit, play with the hay,
and flourish generally after the manner
of boys, and to run about the old-fash-
ioned house with its many curious nooks
and kindly faces.

Rossie had a well-founded idea that his grandpapa was one of the best men in the world, and began very young to imitate him as far as he could, thinking that, if he was so good, it would be good in a little boy to kneel like him, to cough like him, to do little things like him. He got at the spirit of it all when he was older. He began to sing before he could talk, and would catch any tune which pleased him by hearing it once or twice, having a great fancy for comic songs. His voice was particularly sweet and musical, and with it he contributed not a little to the enjoyment of his friends. He always showed a desire to act out the stories he heard, and when very young, in repeating the story of Samuel and Eli, would always try to imitate a man's voice in the call, " Samuel, Samuel,"

and then in a child's voice, call out
"Here am I." As he grew older, he
learned a great deal of poetry, which he
repeated with dramatic emphasis and
action. When a very little boy, he liked
to say "Poor Peter," which we will give
for the amusement of other little folks : —

"Poor Peter was burnt by the poker one day,
    When he made it look pretty and red;
  For the beautiful sparks made him think it fine play,
    To lift it as high as his head.

"But somehow or other, his finger and thumb
    Were terribly scorched by the heat,
  And he screamed out aloud for his mother to come,
  And he stamped on the floor with his feet.

" Now if Peter had minded his mother's command,
    His fingers would not have been sore;
  And he promised again, as she bound up his hand,
    To play with hot pokers no more."

When he came to,

    " His finger and thumb
  Were terribly scorched by the heat,"

he would put out his finger and thumb
with an expression of great pain, and at

" Stamped on the floor with his feet,"

he would stamp violently.

While he was a little fellow, he took a
journey with his mother, and was on the
ocean for the first time ; he stood lean-
ing over the side of the boat, looking
down into the water very sedately
awhile, then turning with a satisfied air,
exclaimed, " Oh, mother, I know what
makes the water so white and foamy ! It
is the salt stirring up from the bottom."

When Rossie was about five years old
his parents thought best to move to a
town at some distance, and he never saw
his grandparents again ; their faithful
service on earth was over, and they soon
went to join the great company in the

"house not made with hands, eternal in the heavens."

As the boy began to make acquaintance with the people in Central Falls, he became specially pleased with Mr. W——, the superintendent of the Sunday-school in which his mother taught the infant class.

One day a merchant near by saw Rossie leading his little dog along the street, and asked him what he was going to do with that dog.

"I'm going to take him to Mr. W—— and have him weighed," answered the child.

"Come in here, my boy, and I'll weigh him for you," said the man.

"No," replied Rossie, "I am going to take him to Mr. W ——; he is the most righteousest man in Central Falls, and he shall weigh my dog."

"But," said the merchant, "I can weigh the dog as well as he can."

"No," persisted Rossie, "I've heard you swear."

So far we have told only of the sunshine. Merry, and making merry, our little boy frolicked gayly through his first five years, never fearing nor feeling the shadow of the cloud into which he was so soon to enter.

How well it is for us who walk this earth in so much weakness that we cannot see just where we are going, or how we shall be led! "Sufficient unto the day is the evil thereof," — sufficient, too, the good that comes with it.

II.

OUR LITTLE BOY'S LOSS AND GAIN.

"There are gains for all our losses,
There are joys for all our pains."

ONE day little Rossie was playing in the barn with some other boys, when his father drove up. The boys wanted to open the door as wide as possible to let him drive in among them, and they pushed as hard as they could; they pushed too hard for the fastenings, and the door fell on our poor little boy.

His father carried him in very carefully, hardly daring to hope that he would ever know him again, but it was not long before he looked up at him and said, " Why, I'm not hurt ; " and in a few days he was able to run about almost as if nothing had happened ; but he never was well after this. He grew thin and pale and very nervous, and was not able to go to school and study like other boys, or even to study at home ; he had attacks of severe pain, which could only be quieted by having his mother clasp him very tightly, and these left him entirely worn out.

At last, about a year after his accident, an abscess formed on his neck, which all the physicians pronounced an indication of spinal disease.

Little Rossie could not run any more now, only walk about slowly and painfully, and there was little hope that he would ever grow better. The abscess, which never healed afterwards, distressed him, and he was a miserable little boy, as he began to think that he might die then, while he knew that he was not prepared to go to heaven.

He had always been a thoughtful child, and knew that he ought to be a Christian; but it was so very easy for him to do wrong that he had never tried long to give up his own way; now it was still easier for him to do wrong, hard to be gentle and patient when he felt so sick and sore, and not to be cross to the other boys who could run about, while he could not, and to be willing to do what others thought best after he had planned for himself; but he thought about the life and death of our Saviour, and prayed for his good Spirit, till the dear Lord gave him strength to try to live like him; and from that time he grew gentler

2

and sweeter. It was still hard for him to be patient and good, but a truly Christian motive had more influence in checking him than any other.

When Rossie was about eight years old, a friend came to visit his mother, and brought a new source of interest for him and his brother on Sunday. He could not read long at a time, because holding a book fatigued him so much, and he was tired of lying and thinking all the day long, so that, though he loved to have Sunday come, he grew weary of the quietness sometimes.

His friend tried to impress the idea upon the boys that Sunday is a gift and a blessing, and ought to be enjoyed thankfully; and to help them to enjoy it, she brought an illustrated edition of the "Pilgrim's Progress," and some picture-cards about it; these never appeared on a week-day, and the boys were so much interested in them, that they were eager, before the week was half through, to have Sunday come, that they might hear how Christian sped on his journey.

"I want to go through the 'Wicket Gate,'" said Rossie, "but I don't care to climb the 'Hill Difficulty;' I'd rather go where I like."

The Hill Difficulty was his appointed path, however, and he walked up it with an increasing faith and trust that made the rough places smooth for him.

Rossie knew that he should never be well again; he was very eager to find out all he could, and, as his father was a physician, he questioned him till he knew quite well the position of all the bones and muscles, and understood ex-

actly where and how he was hurt. At
first, he was very much troubled, for fear
his mother would die and leave him, and
found it hard to feel that God would
take care of him, if he should take her
away. Not that she was sick at all,
but the little boy's mind was apt to dwell
on painful subjects, and his dependence
on his mother made him think how
much he should miss her if she should
leave him.

He could not study regularly, because
his brain was easily excited, but as he
had a very good memory, and was always asking sensible questions, he con-
trived to learn so much that he seemed
much older than he really was, and he
had such a comically wise way of putting
things, that older people liked to talk
with him, so he had an opportunity of

learning more and more every day. He
learned to write well, though he had to
hold his poor head with one hand, and
he found great comfort in drawing, for
which he had a natural taste. About
this time, " The Pearl of Orr's Island" was
coming out in the " Independent,"and he
illustrated the weekly numbers in a very
spirited style, spending hours in drawing
the figures on his porcelain slate. He
could sew, too, making a tiny patch-work
bed-quilt, and doing some pieces of wors-
ted-work, always busy about something,
when he was at all able to be employed.

But with all the amusements that he
could have, and nothing reasonable was
ever denied to the little sick boy, it was
a great trial to be sick; he had been
a very active child and eager to learn;
now he could only look at the others

racing about, while he moved slowly wrapped in his dressing-gown, from one place to another, and he was only able to study for a few moments at a time; besides, his disease was one that makes its victims irritable, and it was not easy for him to be pleasant and amiable, though he tried.

Much of the joy of life had passed away from him, but he had received a great blessing, — so great a one that he felt afterwards thankful for the injury which had turned his thoughts to the Saviour; his trust in him was as an anchor that never failed him, and he was sure that all the pain was sent by the overruling Love. So while we pitied poor little Rossie, we were glad for him, for he knew the meaning of life, and learned its lessons well and deeply. If his path did lie up the Hill Difficulty, he saw many things that were hidden to the dwellers on the plain, and all the shadows never veiled the Great Sun from his childish eyes.

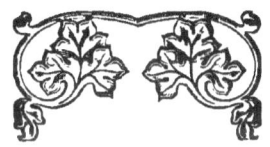

III.

NEW FRIENDS.

"Through losses and crosses,
Be lessons right severe;
There's wit there, ye'll get there,
Ye'll find nae other where."

WHEN Rossie was about ten years
old, his father's mother was very
sick, and his mother made her a long
visit, so he was sent to pass some time
with an aunt who was boarding in the
same town where he had so loved to
visit his grandpapa. He soon became
acquainted with all the neighbors, and,
with a little relative about his own age,
used to go in and out through the great
farmhouses, with "the comfortable easi-
ness of childhood." They liked to go

into the graveyard, too, and think and
talk soberly, not sadly, of the friends
who were buried there. So knowledge
and love of both the living and the dead
grew stronger in them as they breathed
the sweet country air, and received those
best gifts that come to us unconsciously.
Sometimes they would ride off to visit a
favorite aunt two or three miles away,
where two cousins were ready to enjoy,
with them, all the wonderful delights of a
great farm, and to introduce them to
horses, cattle, pigs, turkeys, hens, and the
whole train of humble friends that glad-
dens the farmyard.

Everybody loved the two delicate
children, and people liked to amuse
themselves with Rossie's " queer streaks "
of knowledge. For instance, he could
tell the history of the translations of the .

Bible quite well, at the same time that he was delighted at learning how to prove addition, and he was always bringing out some bit of information that was odd for a child to have. He was still very fond of singing, though his voice had lost somewhat of the peculiar sweetness which had marked it. His favorite hymn at this time was

> "Must Jesus bear the cross alone,
>   And all the world go free?
> No, there's a cross for every one,
>   And there's a cross for me.
>
> " How happy are the saints above
>   Who once went sorrowing here!
> But now they taste unmingled love,
>   And joy without a tear.
>
> "The consecrated cross I'll bear,
>   Till death shall set me free,
> And then go home my crown to wear;
>   For there's a crown for me."

This hymn he used to apply to himself and his friends most appropriately, showing a quickness of thought and perception wonderful in a child so young.

A Pomfret friend writes, "He chose for me the hymn, 'Must Jesus bear the Cross alone?' After I had played it for him, he said, referring to an invalid friend in the house, 'We all know what Miss H——'s cross is, but what is yours?' Then seeing my eyes fill with tears, he added, 'Ah, I think Miss C——'s thoughts trouble her sometimes,' looking at me *so* pityingly all the time. I involuntarily drew the little face near to me, and kissed him, and thought the cross he bore, which to many might have seemed *too* heavy, had not crushed out large sympathy for others, — nay, had taught it.'

In fact, he was a singular mixture of child and man. While he liked to play

with paper dolls, on wet days when he
could not go out, he liked better to visit
his grandpapa's minister, and talk with
him of Jesus and of heaven, enjoying his
society as much as that of his playmates.
The good man says of him, " He was a
wonder to me; he was one of those children, of whom the prophet says, that,' one
shall die an hundred years. old;' his
mind appeared to be occupied with the
gravest subjects, and his· reasonings to
have the maturity and strength of age,.
while in many respects he was altogether
a child."

The young pastor, whose church he
attended, boarded in the same family,
and the children were careful not to dis-
turb him when busy, though they were
fond of visiting his room at proper times.
Mr. A——— writes, " I saw much of him in

the summer of 1862, while a pastor in Pomfret. For many weeks we eat at the same table, and slept beneath the same roof, and many times in the day exchanged greetings, which were often prolonged, when my duties would warrant me the pleasure of inviting him to my study, into the free and informal interview of an hour. My impressions of him are very vivid, as a boy of singular maturity of character and early development of mind, united with the utmost simplicity and trustfulness, at an age which to many is but the dawning of mature thought and reflection upon the grave questions of religious faith. His mind was quick to perceive the truth, not in its abstract form, like the existence of a God, and his right to govern the world, but in its relations to himself, grasping

the thought of God as his Father, and
Jesus as his Saviour, and his duty to
live a holy and obedient life. With all
his maturity of mind, he never lost the
element of childhood.

" Of the many interviews, which are associated in my mind with Rossie's life in
Pomfret, I remember one with great dis-
tinctness. I think it was near the time
of our communion that he came to my
room, and greeting me in that sweet
way that was peculiar to him, asked me
if I were disengaged. I told him, ' Yes,
if Rossie wished to see me.' He said he
wished to talk with me about making a
profession of his faith in Christ. In answer to my inquiries, he told me of the
time when he gave his heart to the Saviour, and how bright and happy his life
had been since he had felt the Saviour's

presence and love in his heart. He spoke
of his first convictions of sin, and his
need of a Saviour, and how he had tried
to obey the Saviour's voice, and go to him
for forgiveness and peace. As an expression of the gratitude and love that
filled his heart, he now desired to make
a public confession of the Saviour, and
his purpose to live to his glory.

"In all the talks I was ever privileged
to have with him, with reference to his
religious life, I never detected in him
anything of self-consciousness. He was
in the most lovely sense a child, early
consecrated, let us hope, to the Master
whose disciple he desired to be. The
memory that will abide with me, when
others grow dim, of our lamented Rossie,
is that of a religious boy, whose heart
beat with warmest love to his Saviour,

who bore the crosses and denials, which
he was pleased to appoint to him, with
singular sweetness and submission, and
who, in the mirror of his affliction, re-
flected the image of his Divine Master."

During this visit, the Sabbath question came up again, as it does in the
education of every child, who is edu-
cated at all in any right sense of the
word. These children were now old
enough to understand why God had said
to them, "Remember the Sabbath-day
to keep it holy;" they had learned that
when God gave his commandments to
Moses, he had called him up into the
stillness of the mountain, that the noise
and cares of daily life might not divert
his attention in the least from the voice
of the Lord Jehovah; they knew that
one of those commandments given so

long ago creates even now such a stillness around our homes on every Sabbath-day; that, without leaving our friends, as Moses did, we, too, can listen undisturbed to his voice. When the coming of our rest-day hushes the busy hum of machinery, shuts the school-house door, takes the tools from the hands of the tired laborer, and relieves the patient cattle, all Christian children know that such changes have a deep and beautiful meaning, and they should see in its restraints the kindness of their heavenly Father in keeping one day for us to learn of him. They know, too, and should always remember, that the ten commandments are so firmly linked together that no one can fail to keep one, and not be likely to break all these inspired laws.

The Sunday-school is a great aid in keeping the minds of the dear little ones interested in the lessons of our Lord, and we know that Jesus, who took young children in his arms and blessed them, will look on it with a sweet and loving smile, and will bless to the teacher and the taught, the good work done for his sake. When our dear Lord was a little boy on our earth, he "kept his Father's law," and he knows the temptations to break it that children have now, and will succor any child who goes to him for strength to do his duty. When he was a man, he told his disciples that though he had come to teach them many new things, he had not come to set aside the ten commandments, and he will be ready to give help to keep them. All God's commands were given us for our

own good, as well as his glory, and a little thought will show any child that our
Lord's day, with all its rest and change
of employment, its heavenly influences,
its higher atmosphere, is an unspeakable
privilege, a precious gift, a wonderful
blessing, a fitting emblem of the rest
above!

Rossie took great interest in tracing
the footsteps of Jesus on the map of Pal-
estine, following his movements on the
hills and through the valleys of Judea
with thorough understanding and sympathy, always interested in whatever
served to illustrate or explain the Bible,
in the study of which he delighted. One
of his favorite expressions in prayer,
which showed the way in which he ap-
plied to his own use what he had learned,
was, "Keep me true to the Bible." He

used to pray a good deal, though he said, "The devil troubles me in praying;" he says, "Get through quick."

At this time, Rossie was asked why he wished to make a profession of religion; he said, "Because I love the Lord Jesus, and wish to obey his commands."

"How do you know that you love him?" was the next question.

"Because I love to please him, and do not do those things I used to which displease him."

"But do you never say or do anything which displeases him now?"

"Certainly I do," replied the little boy, "but I am very sorry when I do so. Before I loved him, I did not care much when I did wrong."

This visit had a good effect on Rossie's health, but the improvement was not lasting. He seemed to look forward quietly to an early death, and often said that he did not see why a Christian should be afraid to die. It was so natural to him to think of religion as the joy of his life that it seemed a part of him which he must express on all suitable occasions. Sometimes it came out oddly half playfully, as in this instance: he was in the habit of adding occasionally " D. V." — *Deo volente,* or " God willing," to a promise or a plan. One day he wrote to a cousin that he had intended to make a visit the day before, but D. wasn't V.

After his grandmother's death, his mother came for him, and he returned to Central Falls, leaving the memory of his little pale face and cheerful patience to the many new friends who had been so kind to him.

IV.

OUR LITTLE PATRIOT.

"We take, with solemn thankfulness,
Our burden up, nor ask it less;
And count it joy that even we
May suffer, serve, or wait for thee,
Whose will be done."

"Nobly borne is nobly done."

WHEN the war, which we all remember so well, — our war, — first broke out, Rossie's father felt that his country called him, and that he must join the army; but how could he leave the poor little sick son, who was so fondly attached to him, and so dependent upon him? He had failed of late, and was growing weaker every day, and it seemed cruel to deprive him of so much happiness, and, at the same time, add to his already painful nervousness.

The struggle was a severe one, but at last the true patriotism that saved our country to us conquered in the family. Rossie, of his own accord, said, " Father, if you think you ought to go, don't stay on my account;" and his father went.

The little patriot bore the parting bravely, but soon began to suffer from the separation and anxiety, and if a letter did not come to reassure them every day, he was too restless to sleep, and his increasing pain told how poorly the weakened nerves were able to bear the strain. How many who were strong to endure the agony of waiting through all that long, dark night of distress and terror, and felt that human strength would sometimes break down under a sudden shock, or the sickening fear that gave them no reprieve, will understand the suffering of the child whose will was strong in the midst of pain, but could not conquer it. Like the martyrs, he could sing psalms in the flames, but was none the less burned.

After some months, the 11th Rhode Island Volunteers, of which his father was surgeon, was ordered to Minot's Hill, near Washington, and Rossie and his mother hastened to join it. The little boy was not able to walk even a few steps to the depot, but every hour seemed to increase his strength as it brought him nearer to his father, and when he arrived at Washington, and met him at last, his joy gave him power for anything, and instead of resting, as had been planned, he rode on in an ambu-

lance at once. Of course every one
feared a reaction, but it never came.
The winter was mild, and Rossie im-
proved every day. His letters, written
while in Virginia, express the greatest
satisfaction "in living in a tent, boarded
up around the sides, with a floor and a
stove." "I had a great deal rather be
here than at home, on account of my
father," writes the boy, who soon grew
well enough to go into the hospital, and
was a great pet of the men. He used to
write letters for them, and amuse them
with his odd, witty sayings, and they
talked to him about their families, and
gave him a share of their good things.

As he grew stronger, his father bought
him an old horse, who seemed to understand the exact state of his rider's nerves,
and was always perfectly gentle with

him; he never even trotted, but walked
carefully about the country when Rossie
was on his back, but as soon as he was
safely on the ground, and one of the
many darkeys had mounted, the animal
relieved himself by innumerable mad
pranks, then he would prick up his ears
and prance, turn round and round, and
start off at full speed, refusing to be quiet
till he had made up for his past self-re-
straint.

The little boy on the large horse was
the subject of occasional jokes from the
soldiers, which he was always ready to
return.

"Hallo, Brigadier General!" called out
one man.

"Hallo, Private!" answered Rossie,
instantly.

"What's your rank?" said another.

"I haven't received my commission yet," was the dignified reply.

Here he had a good lesson in politeness, which may be useful to some other little boy. He had visited the headquarters of the medical director, which were also those of Gen. Abercrombie, with his father, and as the director liked to talk with him, he went often. One day he went alone, and saw an old man in faded dressing-gown and shabby slippers, reading his paper at a window, but took no notice of him. In the course of a chat with the director, Rossie suddenly said, "Does Abercrombie live here in this house?" and was going on to express his desire to see him, when a significant gesture made him look at the old man, who had dropped his paper, and was peering at him over his spectacles.

" Who is this young gentleman ? " said he, in a deep voice.

"It is Surgeon Perry's son," said the director.

Poor Rossie was ashamed of himself for once, and declared that he should never forget to put the handle on any one's name as long as he lived, though he would persist that " a Major General, if he did not choose to wear his uniform, ought at least to look decent."

Rossie was devoted to President Lincoln with the enthusiasm of a child and a patriot. He was taken to Washington to attend two of the public receptions, and was delighted to see the kindly face, which smiled its peculiar, sad smile on the pale, eager one upraised to it. He liked to see the public buildings, but the Dead Letter Office had a special fascina-

tion for him ; he cried himself sick at seeing the heaps of letters and gifts sent to
dead or missing soldiers, but he always
wanted to go again; his sympathy for all
our heroes knew no bounds.

During the last part of the winter,
Rossie was delighted by the coming
of his brother, whose presence always
doubled his enjoyment and alleviated his
sufferings, and the two used to go out on
little expeditions to rebel camps and
other points of interest, returning with
many trophies. The negroes were a
never-failing source of interest to the
boy, who treated them with the greatest
kindness, and made great efforts to teach
them. He took much pains with a very
odd boy, " half-boy and half-monkey," full
of mischief, named Crash, an unpromising
subject, who would not be taught, but

was always ready to dance and sing. He had a special fondness for what he called "leegious" (religious) songs, of which the following may serve as a specimen: —

> "I had a little sisser,
> And she got 'verted;
> I had an ole mudder
> Come a runnin' wid de news.
> Jesus, Jesus,
> Am sittin' on God's throne."

A more hopeful pupil was Amos, a black preacher, earnest and devoted, but very ignorant. He begged to be taken North when the doctor returned, so that Rossie had an opportunity of teaching him to read and write somewhat, and it would be difficult to tell whether pupil or teacher was most delighted when Amos finished, without assistance, his first sentence, "I am a free man."

Rossie had been examined for admission to the church before he left home, and, as no one had any doubt of his faith in Christ and even maturity of religious experience, he would have been received by the family of believers at that time, had he not left home so suddenly to join his father. While he was with the army, he told the chaplain of the regiment of this, and expressed his very strong desire to be admitted to the Communion, which was accordingly done, and he joined, for the first time, in the outward sign of remembrance of the Saviour, whom he had long loved.

The chaplain says of him, " He was with us during three or four months of the winter of 1862–63, and he endeared himself to all with whom he associated. He took special delight in whatever touched the great questions of freedom and education for the slaves, and in the religious interests of the regiment. At our evening meetings, his camp-chair was usually near my own, and there was no heart more in sympathy with the service, no eye oftener filled with tears, no voice more sweetly blended with our songs. Often was I delighted to converse with him of religious trust and joy; his experience seemed to be that of a mature Christian."

A letter from Rossie's mother, about this time, tells of one of those sudden movements, incident to camp life, so graphically, that we need no excuse for inserting it. "And now I must tell you of the most serious experience of camp life I've yet met with. On Sunday night we ladies, three in number, went out to dress-parade, because in pleasant weather the religious services are held immediately after in the open air. It was like a summer evening; the sky was as red and glowing as it is with us in August, and the air almost as mild. The regiment never looked better, and, as they all joined in singing the doxology, I thought I never heard anything finer; I remarked to Mrs. G——, the chaplain's wife, that the more I saw of them, and the more perfect they became in their exercises, the more I dreaded the thought of their being called upon to lay down their lives on the battle-field.

"We went to bed as usual, but, about midnight, what they call the LONG-ROLL was sounded. It was an awfully solemn sound, breaking as it did so suddenly on the perfect stillness, though I had no idea what it meant till the doctor jumped up, and in a moment more the whole camp was alive; it was a warning that the rebels were near, and in a moment more came the order to march with knapsacks and blankets, and everything on their backs. Signal-rockets had been thrown up, and the whole brigade was ordered to march no one knew where, or whether it would ever come back again. The colonel left the surgeon in charge of the sick, and told him to be in readiness to attend the wounded, if there was an engagement, and the quarter-master was left in care of the stores, and both were left in charge of the camp, with forty men as guard.

"All the brigade formed into line on the parade-ground; all seemed in good spirits; it was a splendid sight. I heard

one man say to Mrs. G——, who was expecting to go to Providence the next
day, 'Tell my wife I went cheerfully:'
another said, 'I would rather my two
boys should live without me under a
good government, than with me under
the Southern Confederacy;' another, a
young man who had made a most impressive prayer at the evening meeting
a few hours before, said to Mrs. G——,
'Give my love to my mother, and tell her
I am not afraid; I am looking up!'

"They marched off singing, 'We are
marching along,' and it was a glorious
sight. We were to remain in camp till
further orders, but to pack up and be
ready to start at a moment's warning.
We went to bed and slept as quietly as
we could under the circumstances, till late
next morning, when I arose and packed

everything of my own and my husband's,
and waited in suspense till late in the day,
when a message came from the colonel
stating that the rebel cavalry had made a
raid, and destroyed some property, but had
passed the place, ten miles off, where our
men went an hour before they arrived.
They were too late to catch the main
body, but I understand they secured two
or three stragglers, and made them pris-
oners, and recaptured some of the stores.
He also sent word that they expected to
return before long. This was a great relief to us, for neither they nor we knew
whether they would come back or not;
but I was glad to see them all back,
I assure you, for I had no fancy for
being *drummed out of camp* in that way.

"The next day all was quiet, but last
night that dreadful LONG ROLL sounded

.again, and the whole brigade received orders to sleep on their arms, and to be ready to march in three minutes' time. They will remain on the alert till further orders.

" We, Rossie and I, had the credit of behaving pretty well in this, to us, rather trying emergency ; but, of course, it is not as if the doctor was obliged to go and leave us. The colonel says his duty is here on account of the sick and wounded, if there should be any.

" At the time of the alarm, Rossie was excited and eager as any of the soldiers, and I really think he expected to go with them. . . . I go down to the hospital as often as I can, write letters for the men, and sometimes make cookies and gingerbread for those who long for something that tastes like home.

One poor fellow has spinal disease, and has suffered awfully. He says, 'I don't know *whom* to send for. When *you* come to see me, I think I want my mother, and when the men have to lift me I want my father.'"

Not long after, it was thought best for Rossie to go home; so the family said good-by to the doctor, and went back again to Central Falls. The change of climate, the new interests, and the different modes of life had worked favorably for the feeble boy, and the improvement was so marked that his parents began to hope that he might yet be spared to them. He himself seemed to have some idea that he might live to grow up, and inquired if he could be allowed to preach sitting down, thinking he should like to be a minister.

The example of a daily effort to conquer all sinful tendencies, and especially to be patient in suffering and confinement, was his allotted way of preaching, and very effective it was. Many of those who knew him write of the powerful impression produced by his cheerful endurance in the midst of such severe pain.

V.

THE SURRENDER.

"I would have gone, God bade me stay;
   I would have worked: he bade me rest.
He broke my will from day to day;
   He read my yearnings unexpressed,
     And said them Nay."

"Heaven is not reached at a single bound,
   But we build the ladder, by which we rise,
   From the lowly earth to the vaulted skies,
    And we mount to its summit round by round."

AS soon as practicable after Rossie's return, he joined the church to which his father and mother belonged, as he had long wished to do. His pastor says of him, "He talked like an old, experienced Christian, and in giving his experience with reference to publicly professing Christ, he was clear and perfectly satisfactory to all who were present; no

one had any question about the genuine-
ness of his faith in Christ, and when he
came forward the next Sabbath, and stood
up before the great congregation, and publicly took upon himself the vows of the
gospel, it was an affecting sight, and one
never to be forgotten by those who wit-
nessed it. We all felt that he would soon
be welcomed to the higher communion
of the spirits of the just in glory.

"He lingered on the shores of time
longer than any of us had dared to hope,
and his room was always a Bethel, the
central place of the family, around which
all the charms of the household seemed
to cluster; but God, at length, took him;
he ripened into heaven; was ready to
go, *glad* to go, and, I have no doubt,
sings the song of redeeming love, with a
strong, unfaltering voice."

Soon after his joining the church, his parents moved to Providence, where the little boy found more objects of interest than he had had before. The family lived for a short time in a large boarding-house, where Rossie made many friends, whom he enjoyed exceedingly. Being decidedly stronger than before he went South, he was able to sew and knit considerably, and amuse himself in many quiet ways. He was always in the habit of riding a great deal with his father, whenever he was at all able, and the beautiful scenery about his new home was a great delight to him. When in the house, he worked with all his strength in making Christmas presents for his friends. After Christmas was over, he commenced a large bed-quilt, made of tiny blocks of silk of various colors, in the arrangement of which he displayed his usual fine taste, varying his employments by knitting and sewing for a little namesake, to whom he wished to make useful presents.

At this time, he had a printing-press, which was a source of very much amusement to him. He printed cards and little sentences, and delighted to send envelopes to his friends, on which he had printed his own name and address, that they might be reminded of his claim to a letter in reply; but it soon appeared, that it was too hard work for him to move the roller, and he was obliged to content himself with arranging the press and setting the type, and to depend on his brother for the printing.

In the course of the summer, Rossie had made some comfort-bags for the soldiers, as so many other boys and girls did during the war, and wrote pleasant little notes with them. A soldier from Massachusetts answered his note, and they kept up a brisk correspondence for some time. Rossie writes, in answer to the first letter:—

"*My dear Friend, Mr. M.,*—I received your letter last Tuesday, and was very glad to get it. I never expected to hear from my comfort-bag, I had waited so long, but 'patient waiters are no losers,' they say, and I believe it; I am glad that the comfort-bag, and the few little things in it, fell into the hands of one that thought the letter worth answering, and if the things have done any good, I should be most happy to send some more; it was a very poor attempt that I made, and I should be glad to better it.

I am a little boy, eleven years old, and I have been sick for six years. I told you that I should like to send you some read ing. What kind of reading do you like? I am a little boy, you know, and I cannot choose reading for grown-up men. Do you like plain, substantial reading, or something like the Waverley Novels? I will send you some religious papers, if you like them.

" My mother was a Massachusetts wo-man, and she says she should like to know any one who comes from that State. My grandfather was a merchant in Boston for thirty or forty years; he was deacon of old Dr. Beecher's church. Perhaps you have heard of him.

" If God spares both our lives, I hope we may meet some time. I shall always be glad I made that comfort-bag, though it was a little thing; it has given me much pleasure in making it, and in hearing from it. I am very glad, Mr. M., that you are a Christian. Perhaps you can, by your letters, help me along. I trust that I am a Christian, though I find it pretty hard to fight the battles sometimes. I hope you will pray for me; I shall always remember you in my prayers. I should really like to hear how many battles you have been in, and all about your life in camp. Did I mention to you, in the little note I wrote, that I spent last winter in camp with my father? We lived under canvas all winter, and had a splendid time!"

Several other letters, full of childish interest and offers of service, followed,

when Rossie was alarmed by some stray
rumors, and wrote, —

"*Dear Friend Joseph,* — I have received no answer to my letter, and we
are all feeling very uneasy about you.
Please drop a line to me, in this envelope, as soon as you receive this. As yet,
I have not heard of the 15th Mass. Regiment being in a fight, but if it has been,
let me know the worst. I do hope and
almost trust that you will come out 'all
right;' but if not, please let me know
the worst, and deliver me from this suspense. Please take means, as I said in
my last, to let me know if you should be
wounded, or anything else."

In the next letter he begs him again
to have him informed of any casualty,

promising to do "everything I can to comfort and help you." After a battle, he writes, " I was exceedingly relieved to get your letter, and know that you came out safe. There was a good deal of assurance in so few words, — 'I'm all right.' That means that you have not been scratched, and have not come very near to being scratched (that is, no nearer than anybody, who goes into a fight, must be). I hope the Lord will be with Joseph, and spare his life all through the campaign. Do take care to have something done, by means of which I can know if you should be *hurt*, — I can't say *killed*. Father, mother, and brother — I haven't any sister (wish I had) — send love, and you know I do."

For some reason, this soldier, though

often invited, never visited Rossie, but he was anxious to receive a visit from him. Rossie promised to go, if he ever got well enough, but he never was so strong again as at that time; so the plan was given up.

As the mild summer weather had strengthened him so much, it was thought best to take him to Boston, to try mechanical means for bringing his spine into natural position, but the attempt was abandoned, after causing him much suffering, and was worse than a failure. The support which was made for him not only gave him very great pain, but caused another abscess, which was even more severe than the first, and never healed while the weary life lasted. The pain and the disappointment were very hard to bear, and poor Rossie's nervous

5

irritability was a great trial both to himself and his friends. On one occasion, after some conversation on the subject of unreasonable exaction had taken place, in his room, he asked a friend if she thought *him* unreasonable. She told him that she did not think he meant to be, but that he was so sometimes. He asked *when,* and she offered to tell him the next time she saw signs of it. He assented, but, with some doubt of his own temper, added, —

"Don't tell me the *same day;* will you?"

Soon after, some one was talking before him about the doctrine of election, or, rather, such misrepresentations of that doctrine as are often made. He listened with great attention, having never been instructed in such matters, and when he

was again alone with his friend, he asked
what the conversation meant, — it was
all new to him. Was there anything in
the Bible about it? Did his grandfather
(his highest human authority) believe
it? His friend was interested to see how
a purely scriptural account of the doctrine would impress a mind like his, and
read to him the last part of the eighth
chapter of Romans, and other kindred
passages, without remark of her own.
He listened with close attention until all
had been read, and then said, —

"Well, if *that* is all any one had to
make such a story out of, I should think
he *wanted* to find fault with God."

This last sentence was uttered very
emphatically.

Rossie had always kept up a great interest in the progress of the war, and had

encouraged the eager, excited communications of the boys of the family, in their frequent visits to his room, keeping himself accurately informed of everything that transpired. At the death of President Lincoln, that great sorrow of our nation, he was overcome with grief, and repeated again and again, —

" Why couldn't God have taken me instead? I am a poor little boy, and can do nothing for my country, and he could do so much."

After this, he positively forbade a word on politics in his room; for he knew that things were going badly, and his weakened nerves could not bear the recital of blunder and wrong-doing.

" I hope," he said, piteously, " the boys wont think I'm not a true patriot; but, indeed, I can't bear to hear them talk about these things now."

The following lines, about the burial of the President, were great favorites with Rossie, who was always ready to read them to his friends : —

" Lay him to rest; lay him deep in the ground.
  Full long enough ye have borne him around,
  With the tramping of horses, the weary drum-beat,
  Before all the eyes and the glare of the street.
                    Lay him to rest.

" They were eyes full of love; they were eyes that did
        weep ;
  And the chillness of death on the cities did creep ;
  But now, let him go, gentle friends, to his rest ;
  Let him go to his home in the heart of the West.
                    Lay him to rest.

• .   .   .   .

" We brought him from westward, because he was just ;
  We made him a chieftain, we gave him our trust ;
  Serene in the midst of the tumult he stood ;
  And we learned that 'tis greatest of all to be good.
                    Lay him to rest.

" We've let him die for us, — yes, we've let him die
  With his armor all on, as the soldier boys lie ;
  Not a moment of warning, — a message to tell ;
  And we say he sleeps well ! and we say he sleeps well !
  Lay him to rest.

" Be proud, Illinois ! for to you it was given
  To raise up the noblest of martyrs for heaven.
  Be pure, Illinois ! for now 'tis your part
  To let the dear ashes repose on your heart.
  Lay him to rest."

At this time, Rossie wrote an account of a sermon from his beloved pastor, which showed the interest and appreciation with which he remembered his words : —

" He compared the two deaths of our Saviour and the President, which the drapings in the house commemorated, — the black drapings on the galleries and pulpit, and the silver vessels and white drapings before the pulpit ; then he spoke of the great likeness and the great

difference ; he said both were assassina-
tions, both were committed by rebels,
and, in both cases, they aimed to destroy
the government they made stronger, and
in both cases they killed their best friend,
and defeated their object. He said the
great difference was, the blood of the
President must be avenged, but the blood
of Jesus was not to bring vengeance, but
pardon and forgiveness." Then, at the last
part of the sermon, he said, " There is
not a man here but feels the sorrow of
these black drapings, and would feel ex-
asperated with any one who could look
with indifference on them ; but have you
nothing to do with these drapings on the
communion-table ? "

Though, on account of his frequent ill-
nesses, Rossie was not able to attend Sunday-school regularly, he was very much

interested in it, and would sometimes in-
sist on going when so weak as to be
obliged to rest on a pillow during the
recitation. He would always learn the
lesson himself, and help the other boys
to do so; then, if he could not go with
them, say, patiently, —

"I shall be with you, in spirit, at
least."

In the summer, he wrote a great many
letters to his brother, who was absent for
some months, giving him graphic ac-
counts of everything that went on at
home, — the fitting of the house, and
consequent hubbub, the freaks of new
horses, etc., illustrating by frequent pen
and ink drawings, wonderfully spirited for
a child. Not long after Grosvenor left,
Rossie wrote to him, —

"*My Dearest Brother,*— . . . I went to the Sunday-School Convention yesterday, the first that has ever been held here, and took the prize offered by Mr. Sargent to the one who could answer his questions. He told a story about two little birds coming and building their nests on the ground, in a large, open field, and the cattle were turned into the field, and they tramped all over the field, and never stepped on the nest, though sometimes they came very near to it; then he said, if any child could give him a passage of Scripture any way like the story, he would give him a book. I waited a few minutes for some one to rise, and then I jumped up and said, as loud as I dared, 'Are not two sparrows sold for a farthing? And one of them shall not fall on the ground without your Father.'

When he came to take my name, he
told me where to go to get the book, and
I shall go to-morrow."

Afterwards he tells him that his prize
book is very interesting, and that Mr.
Sargent wrote him a letter, to which he
replied.

Many things in the simple, free letters
of Rossie show how completely religion
had become a part of his inner life; he
begs Grosvenor not to delay attending to
it, and wishes that he were ready to join
the church to which he and their parents
were about to unite themselves.

A good place had been found for Amos
with one of Rossie's aunts, where he was
well cared for. Rossie writes to his
brother, —

" If you write to Amos, be sure to form every letter correctly, or he cannot read them ; and make your R's like this (*r*), for he cannot read the other kind (r). You had better direct an envelope to yourself, and enclose it to him, and tell him what to do with it, for he wont suffer Aunt M. to direct his letters, and don't know how himself, though he thinks he does."

Amos was so anxious to learn more, that he went to the district school for three successive winters, and studied with the children till he could read and write well.

White ("my young missis call me White, 'cause I so black ") was another *protegé* of the doctor who had been brought from the army, and was retained in the family ; he was very faithful and devoted to Rossie, who writes of him, " White gets along nicely with his studies. I am trying to teach him figures; he knows them as far as nine, but can't go two figures. I think he will learn in a little while. He is getting quite independent, and I am glad of it. He does not seem at all afraid of any one now, though he is just as ready to do what we ask him as he ever was."

In July, Rossie writes, —

"*My Own Darling Brother,*—I have been very sick, and can hardly say I'm any better now, though I have got into a good position in my chair, and am not in so much pain as I have been. This is a comfortable day, and I wish I could jump up and go down street in the horse-cars; but, oh! if I move an inch in my chair,

I am in terrible pain. Another abscess is forming, and there is no putting it off; it is coming slowly but surely. I don't think it will have to be lanced, for it must be about ready to break now, so I expect to be spared that agony. Our friends are going away, and I shall be so glad to have you home so soon to comfort and amuse me."

He was soon rejoiced by the home-coming of the brother whom he had so much missed, who shared his interests and devoted himself to his comfort. He writes to another friend, —

" You can't think how glad I was to see Grosvenor; I never was so long away from him before. Only think, I did not see him in six months; he is now in college, having passed a first-rate examination. He has joined a society which is not a wholly ' good-time ' society, but is for mutual improvement. He has told them about his resolution not to smoke, nor drink anything; they congratulated him, and said they would not tempt him."

Rossie had been sick so long, and was, withal, such a decided character, that he often talked as if the older of the two, and Grosvenor listened good-naturedly, with all deference. Rossie once heard a minister talking with one of his friends of the little feeling of their own sinfulness exhibited by some who professed to be Christians, remarking that the preaching of the present day, unlike that of a former period, was calculated to produce such a result; and not long after, he inquired of this friend what the minister meant. He was told that he probably meant that unless one felt that he was a great sinner he would not feel his need of the Saviour of sinners. His brother, who was present, said that his pastor had told him that he must not wait to feel his sinfulness any more, but must now consecrate his life to the Saviour, but that he thought he was not ready to do *that*, because he had not a deeper sense of his guilt.

"But," said Rossie, "as Jesus Christ *has* died for you, why not accept what he *has* done, as he asks you to, and spend your time in trying to do better?"

Rossie knew very well that he was sicker than he had been, yet he had no fear of death. He was by no means a perfect boy, and did not consider him-

self at all so ; but he knew that he wished
to do right, and tried to be good and patient, and he knew, too, that the loving
Saviour could see that he wanted to be
like him, and would help him, as he will
help any boy or girl who tries to do his
will.

This knowledge made our poor sick boy
able to bear so much pain, and gave him
more happy thoughts in all his suffering
than many healthy children have who
never felt his distress or his consolation.
He could say truly, —

> " To-day, ay, even this very hour
>   *Is the best hour I ever knew.*
> Not that my Father gives to me
>   More blessings than in days gone by,
> Dropping in my uplifted hands
>   All things for which I blindly cry,
> But that his plans and purposes
>   Have grown, to me, less strange and dim,
> And, where I cannot understand,
>   I trust the issue unto Him."

VI.

ESAU.

"A bundle of possibilities, tied up with mischief."

" But our captain counts the image of God nevertheless his image, cut in ebony as if done in ivory." — THE GOOD SEA CAPTAIN.

E have got a strange addition to our family in the shape of a ten-year-old black boy," writes Rossie, " as smart as a cricket, and quick as lightning. Papa found him in the hands of a police officer, and offered to take him, and care for him; so he brought him home here, and now he seems quite at home.

"Perhaps you may think as I did, 'What in the world can we do with him?' He has found plenty to occupy his time since he came, principally in waiting upon me, setting and waiting on table, which he does to a T, running to the door, etc.; he is very smart, as I say, and I only wish he had you to teach him; he knows nothing at all of 'book-larnin';' don't know who Jesus Christ is, or anything at all about the Bible; he don't know three weeks from three years, and in fact hardly knows anything of that sort, but he is very quick, and has learned a verse in the Bible very well in a short time."

To his brother he writes, "Papa has concluded that crutches would help. me about walking, and take the pressure off my spine. I am inclined to think so too, though I declare I never will be seen in the street with them.

"Well, papa said he would try and get

some, so he went off in the morning after taking the measure for the crutches, and about half an hour afterwards he drove up to the door again, and came up the front steps, where I met him. 'Look here,' said he, 'I've brought you some *legs*, Rossie.' Well, it was very natural for me to think he had brought the crutches, but while I was looking round for them, he turned my head in the right direction, and, lo, and behold! 'what do you think I saw?' Nothing more nor less than a little coal-black boy about my size. Papa introduced me to him in the following manner : —

" ' You see him ? '

" ' Yar, sar.'

" ' Well, that's your master. You understand ? '

" ' Yar, sar ' (with a very broad grin),

after which introduction, he asked me what I thought of my legs. I told him I was sure *I* did not know what to do with him.

"'Well,' he said, 'a policeman was taking him off to the Reform School, and I offered to take him; so he let me bring him home here, and now he will wait on table, go to the door, and wait on you in particular, and you must teach him to read.' So we brought him in, put on some decent clothes, and he was duly installed."

When the queer-looking little boy first came, Rossie asked his name.

"Esau Lee, sir," was the reply.

Various other questions being answered he looked at the boy thoughtfully, and said, "Well, Esau, you find the legs, and I'll find the brains;" but he found himself

excused from that care, for Esau had
plenty of brain, though it was sadly in
want of guidance. He had run away
from his master, and had followed a regiment to Providence. On his way thither,
he had learned a great many funny
tricks, with which he used to amuse the
soldiers, being rewarded with whiskey or
a little money, and he liked these much
better than doing anything sensible.
He had no idea of the rights of property,
and Rossie insisted that " he didn't know
how to speak the truth ; " but he soon had
a warm attachment to his young "massa," as he called him, and " massa's " care
and love acted powerfully to restrain the
wild little waif.

Nothing could be known of Esau's
mother, as neither he nor any of the
soldiers knew where his master lived, so

no inquiries could be made. The boy
seemed to remember her lovingly, sometimes saying, when looking at the moon,
" My mudder see dat moon," and object-
ing to have his hair cut or his name
changed, lest his " mudder nebber know
him." Frequently when he had fallen
into disgrace, he was heard to soliloquize
in a corner, " Silly boy to run away from
mudder ! "

At first, Esau had a trick of hiding, if
he did not choose to answer any call, ap-
parently imagining that no one would
have energy enough to hunt him up; but
he soon found his mistake, and became
tolerably obedient. He was a firm be-
liever in ghosts when he came, and was
sure that he had seen them, but finally
concluded that it was his " mudder " who
had had that pleasure. Rossie tried to

convince him that it was impossible, asking him if he did not know that his soul would go either to heaven or to hell, and his *body* .only would be buried, when he died, and that couldn't walk about the graveyard to frighten people ; for after the flesh had become dust, it would be like " Qld Dess " [Old Death], as Esau always called the skeleton in the doctor's office. " Yes," said he, " I know that only my *meat* will be put in the ground," but seemed to have some idea that the spirits of the wicked walked the earth perhaps as a punishment.

Esau was very much affected by the story of Jesus Christ, as told him by Rossie, who took great pains to make him understand the account of the crucifixion, and the idea that Jesus was willing to endure it all to save him. Being asked afterwards, "Why he should try to please God?" he readily answered, as if there could be but one reply to such a question, "Oh, 'cause he let his Son die for me."

When Esau came into the family, Rossie was much affected by his utter ignorance of spiritual things, and taught him as his first prayer, the cry of the blind man by the wayside, "Jesus, thou Son of David, have mercy on me."

He always taught him his Sunday-school lessons faithfully, and instructed him about his duties to others. He overheard him at one time joining with other boys in calling wicked names, and told him that he must not do so.

"Yes, Massa Rossie, I shall call him all the names I ever can, 'cause he call me *bery* bad words."

"But," said Rossie, "Jesus did not do so when people called him bad names, and he didn't teach us to do so."

"Massa Rossie," replied Esau, impatiently, "Jesus Christ was *Jesus Christ*, but we's only peoples."

Esau was sensitive about his color, and came in one day, complaining bitterly that some one had called him a "nigger." Rossie told him that it meant negro, and was used as the Irish are called Paddies, and he himself a Yankee, adding, "I don't mind when they call me Yankee, and you must not mind when they call you nigger."

"Well," said Esau, somewhat abashed, and trying to excuse his anger, "I told him I didn't come to *him* to make me white."

One day he was found cutting his hair

in a peculiar way, and explained that he was trying "to cut a *path* in it like Massa Rossie's." He inquired of White, "What for your hair and mine not like Massa Rossie's?"

"Oh, go 'way," was the unsatisfactory reply. "What for your mudder' and mine not like Massa Rossie's?"

At another time a man, passing the two boys, heard Esau say, "Massa Rossie," as he always did, and inquired, "Is *that* little fellow your master? and do you have to mind him?"

After he had passed, Rossie said, "*You* don't care, Esau; do you?"

"I don't care about the *mind*, Massa Rossie, but I does care about the *little*."

"Dat boy," as White used to call him, mixed up his bits of information in a very funny way sometimes. Being asked in Sunday-school "how God put a soul into Adam at the creation?" he very soberly said, "He *blew* it into him."

He was at one time informing White of a new bit of knowledge he had gained, asking him if he knew that the abbreviation Mr. meant a gentleman. White asked him what Mrs. meant.

"Why, if Mr. means one gentleman, Mrs. means *two* gentlemen, sure."

Like most of his race, he liked the sound of long words, and was not particular to understand their meaning. One day he heard some one say, in answer to a question, that the doctor was engaged.

"Yes, missis," said he, "the doctor is in de gage ob de cow now."

Finding that much was thought of birthdays, he concluded to have his on the same day with Rossie, and to call himself twelve when Rossie was fourteen ; and after this was settled between them, Esau quietly remarked that he thought the doctor would have the bells rung on the occasion, but was told that they were neither of them of sufficient importance in the community for such a demonstration. Unexpectedly to the family, in the course of the day the bells did ring for the inauguration of Gen. Burnside as Governor of Rhode Island, when Esau ran in, much delighted, saying he "knowed the doctor would have de bells rung."

Rossie took much care of Esau, who committed to him the charge of his purse, and other equally important trusts. One day, after he had been particularly disobedient, Rossie handed him some new clothes which had been made for him, with the question, —

" Do you think you deserve these, Esau? Have you behaved well enough to have them?"

"I don't *'have* for dem t'ings, Massa Rossie; I *works* for 'em," was his reply.

In the midst of his own pain, Rossie used to pray and work for Esau, who always knew where he could find sympathy and advice in his many distresses, and his still more frequent scrapes, and being the younger, though much the larger of the two boys, was willing to learn from him. Though Rossie was sometimes impatient with his waywardness, he was generally considerate towards him; he taught him as far as he had strength, and prayed often and earnestly for his conversion, sending a message from his death-bed, to tell Esau that he *must* be a Christian.

VII.

OUR LITTLE MAN.

" All may be heroes: —
' The man who rules his spirit,' saith the voice
Which cannot err, ' is greater than the man
Who takes a city.' Hence it surely follows,
If each might have dominion of himself,·
Then each would be a prince, a hero, — greater,
He will be a Man, in likeness of his Maker."

N the winter of 1865–66, the doctor's house was the home of several cousins, all boys, attending school or college, full of eager, busy life. Rossie was interested in all they said and did, but he was such a care-taking child, and so full of nervous anxieties about them, that his father thought his health might improve if he would withdraw from the household, and only see the family as they

called at his room. He told the boy that
he would live longer if he should do so.
But this was no motive to him; and since
he was already shut out from so many
sources of entertainment, and his life was
likely to be so short, both father and
mother felt unwilling to oblige him to
retire from the family.

His aunt tried to persuade him to take
his room voluntarily, promising to remain with him and share his confinement, and urging that he could preserve
a more Christ-like spirit in a more quiet
life. This struggle was a severe one;
there was much for him to give up, and
the result was somewhat uncertain. He
had been able to ride, and would even
go by himself in the street cars, over-
taxing entirely his slender strength, and
returning exhausted and irritable; but as

his retirement to his room included the
experiment of temporary confinement to
his bed, this great pleasure would be entirely cut off, as well as the amusement
of seeing all the callers in a very lively
family. Then he had a great desire to
be remembered always, and feared that
when he should be out of sight, some
one of his many cherished friends might
not think of him so often, or so tenderly,
as before. The decision was left to himself, and he finally concluded, after
thoughtful and prayerful deliberation,
that it was God's will that he should give
up his own will in the matter, and retire
to his room. After he had once made up
his mind, he had no more doubt, and said,
a few days later, "I feel more as if I were
doing as God would have me do than I
have for a long time." He chose his

own room, received the promise of each one of the family not to forget him, and to visit him often, and passed heroically from them to his bed.

The resolution which had been so hard for him introduced a new era in his character. Ever after he was more manly, more self-contained, more watchful over his temper, and more anxious to do *just* the will of his heavenly Father; and he would often ask at night whether he had exercised self-control during the day, and speak of the effort it cost him, showing how closely he watched his own emotions. At this time, he wrote, —

"You may have heard that I am now confined to my chamber, also to my bed; not that I am much worse, though I think my spine is more curved than it used to be, so that papa thought, if

7

something were not done immediately, I couldn't live long. After some persuasion, and quite a struggle in my own mind, I concluded *to go to bed.* I said, when I came, that I would stay a month. Three weeks of it have gone; of course I shall not get up at the end of the month. Now that I have begun, I shall lie till some permanent good comes from it; that is, unless I find, at the end of six months, that I am no better. I think, though, that I am already better, so that I hope to get up in the spring or early summer. It is a great trial to me, but all my friends are very kind, especially Aunt L——, who has given up all her plans, just to come and take care of me. . . . . But you must excuse me from writing more now, for it is hard to write on one's back, — and write soon, and amuse and please your bedridden little friend,

"R. P. P."

From this time, Rossie's room was a good place for the other boys, where they talked over their plans and difficulties, and found the constant help of his practical common sense. Many cases of conscience were settled there, and many an impulse to earnest, manly Christian life came from the child, whose life of trial and suffering drew slowly nearer its close. He was anxious that his room should be cheerful to them, that they might remember it with pleasure after he had gone.

The first call he received there was from his pastor, with whom he talked about his decision, and Dr. S. confirmed him in the idea that he had indeed followed God's will, by complying with the expressed wishes of his friends and doctors, as really as if it had been made known in another way.

Rossie's room and appointments were chosen by himself. He used a soldier's cot, having on one side a writing-desk, well supplied with paper and envelopes of various sizes, pens, pencils, paints, stamps, drawing paper, and sealing-wax, and containing four motto cards, placed by himself on each corner of the lid : "For me to live is Christ, and to die is gain." "Thy will be done on earth." "By the grace of God, I am what I am." "Looking unto Jesus." On the other side was a work-table provided with scissors, needles, pins, silk, and thread of all imaginable varieties (for he was still able to embroider very nicely, and made beautiful presents of his own handiwork to his friends). Two large scrolls, one of Bible verses, one of devotional poetry, hung in his room, and were regularly turned for him.

For some weeks Rossie lay patiently on his little bed, but the position aggravated his cough so much that the experiment was given up, and he began to move about and sit in a low rocking chair as before; but he remained confined to that one room for several months.

He would take his little portfolio on his knees and write for some time, expressing himself with great clearness and ease; or he would paint, draw, or embroider, showing in all the nicest taste, till the bright scarlet spot on his cheek gave warning that his strength was overtaxed. His care for the family was as marked as ever; he insisted on keeping the tools used in the household in his own room, because the boys would leave them about, and no one would know where they were, while he could take care of them and make the others bring back what they had used.

While confined to his room, he writes to a friend, "I do know that I am a thousand times better off than thousands of people both poor and rich. Don't think that I think my cross so heavy; it is not. I think I have borne heavier myself; I should not have to go to Boston, or among your poor people, to find much greater sufferers than myself. One poor woman — not poor as far as money goes — is very much worse than I am, for she has not lain down for two or three weeks.

She has dropsy, and has to sit straight up in a chair, all the time. I myself, when my first abscess came, suffered ten times worse than I do now. For twenty days I could neither sit nor lie, but had to rest in mother's lap, my knees on her knees and my head on her shoulder; I used to lie for hours dreading to stir, and when I did have to move, oh, what agony I suffered! And then the lancing! Oh, I am quite well off now; I have everything for my comfort. These scrolls — one of beautiful hymns, the other of comforting texts — hang where I read them twenty times a day.

"My little table by my bed has two glass dishes full of the most lovely green-house flowers on it, and almost always I have them through the kindness of friends. Papa has just bought me a

Waltham watch, so that I can always know the time. Auntie reads beautiful stories, etc., etc. It makes my confinement much easier, though it is pretty tiresome now. I am better than when I came up, and hope to be about by the time roses are in bloom."

He was orderly by nature, and it seemed best and pleasantest to plan a regular course of occupations and amusements for the day, though, on account of his increasing pain and weakness, these plans " were made of leather not of iron ; " still he was happier to have some order to fall back upon. He could not begin his day early, as his nights often gave him but little repose, but as soon as possible after breakfast he listened to the reading of God's Word, which, he said, was " the most interesting thing he did in the day." To him the Bible was a book of deep and never failing interest; he learned about its history, and the way in which God had preserved it to us; he followed step by step the movements of God's chosen people, and still more intently the footsteps of the Divine Master, while he drew nearer day by day to the final union with him. On one occasion, his pastor found little Rossie much disturbed by the recurrence of bleeding at the nose, and saying that he could not feel resigned to it. Dr. Swain asked if he had prayed that it might be taken away.

" Oh, yes," said Rossie, " indeed, I have."

"That is right," replied the doctor. "Jesus prayed that the cup might pass away, but he said something else, too: 'Nevertheless, not my will, but thine be

done.'" Rossie remembered that he had
asked only for relief, and confessed his
mistake.

One day he spoke of his clothing,
which was merely a night-gown, saying, "When I get well, I'm not going to
dress as I do now; I shall dress very
nicely."

He then went into a minute description of each separate article of a boy's ap-
parel, which he meant to have, convers-
ing in such animated strains that it was
almost painful to listen, when one knew
how little likely he was ever to wear
such clothes. All at once his tone
changed, and he said, "But I shall not
need the clothes. I am not going to get
well; I'm going to another country."

"Then," said his friend, "you'll wear
a white robe, and have palms in your

hands," alluding to a verse on the scroll in his room.

"Yes," said he, "and then I shall walk in the golden streets, and see Jesus and the angels, and grandpa and grandma and my little brother (one who had died in infancy), and all whom I know in heaven."

His voice faltered, he threw his arms around her, and burst into tears, and said, "*I* don't know why it is, when I want to go to heaven *so much*, that I can't speak of it without tears, but I believe it is the *separation*."

After a conversation on the shortness of the dreaded separation, he was comforted. Though racked with suffering, Rossie was ready to sympathize with every one of his many visitors, and had a rare tact in choosing the subjects best calculated to entertain them. Boys and girls liked to go to his pleasant room, and older people, too, found pleasure there. He had many kind friends, his pastor was most attentive, and ever gladly welcomed. His brother and cousins were devoted to him, and nothing was wanting that could cheer his hours of retirement. Still, though patient, he was very tired of the winter's confinement; and near its close, he writes, "I am quite contented now, and have not the slightest desire to be out in the wind and cold; but I should like to go over the house into all the rooms, and see how they have got along without me. I sometimes think I might do a great deal more if I could go about, that is, be more useful; but they all think this is my duty, and I suppose I shall 'stick it out' now to the end of the six months. I try to do some good to the two contrabands that are here; they have taken a new start since Aunt L—— took hold with me, and I think both will soon be able to read right off in any book. But I must wind up my precious watch and go to bed. This going to bed is in reality getting out of bed, having my bed made, and getting in again."

"My poor little boy," said his father, "you must have a weary life of it; you have suffered more than any boy I ever knew."

"But you must remember, father," said the little invalid, "that if I have suffered more, I have enjoyed more, too."

One night, after he had gone to bed, he said, "Auntie, I shall always thank God that he made me a sick little boy, for I think I should have been a very wicked one if he had not."

His aunt tried to quiet him, fearing that, if he talked, he would be too much excited to sleep, but he was anxious to confess something " very wicked," which he had once done. Not receiving an immediate answer to his confession, he said, anxiously, "Auntie, are you *very sorry* I told you?" evidently fearing that the love he prized so highly would be diminished. Being reassured on this point, and reminded of the scriptural injunction, ' Confess your faults one to another, and pray one for another," he was very desirous to know *how* he was to be certain that he had repented, since it was unlikely that he would be ever tempted to sin in the same way again.

" Repentance is to leave
The sins we loved before;
And show that we in earnest grieve
By doing so no more."

This was Rossie's idea of repentance, — he was simply amazed at being sometimes spoken to as if his willingness to die arose from an innocent life; for he knew that he had often done wrong, had often been irritable and exacting, but he felt sure of his heavenly Father's love to him, and of his longing desire to forgive every offence. He could go to him in penitence, saying, "I have sinned," and enjoy a sense of his forgiveness, while growing more and more anxious to avoid his besetting sins, and to bring forth fruits worthy of repentance.

Rossie had the utmost faith in prayer, and his petitions for all the younger members of the family were very earnest, but for his only brother they were truly importunate. He prayed, as if he could not be denied, that he might love the Saviour, and that, together with their parents, they might sit at his table, and commemorate his love. Rising from his knees, he once cast his eyes upon the scroll of Bible verses, and read the following: "If two of you shall agree on earth, as touching anything which they shall ask, it shall be done for them of my Father which is in heaven."

"Is that verse certainly true?" he asked. "Does God mean *just* as he says?"

"Certainly," was the reply.

"Then," continued he, "I feel sure that Grosvenor will be converted, for you and I are two, and we certainly do agree about this one thing."

After this, he was constantly watching for an answer to his prayer, hailing with gratitude his brother's increasing interest in the great subject, and grieving if he noticed that anything else was occupying too much of his thought.

8

VIII.

FARTHER ON.

"Closer and closer my steps
Come to the dark abysm,
Closer Death to my lips
Presses the awful chrism.

"Oh, happy, happy that I am !
If thou canst be, O Faith,
The treasure that thou art in life,
What wilt thou be in death?"

SOON after he wrote to the friend who had prayed with him, "Our prayers are answered, and Grosvenor is a Christian; he is going to join the church here, and father, mother, and myself all join it too, from the church in Central Falls. Then we shall be an unbroken family at the Lord's table."

The union for which he had longed so

earnestly and prayed so ardently had at
last taken place, and when the summer
weather permitted our sick boy to go out
again, the whole family went together to
commemorate the love which illumined
alike the active, busy life of the mature,
the earnest, preparatory work of the in-
genuous youth, and that slow and solemn yet cheerful approach to the grave
which made the sick-room a Bethel.

After this Rossie was taken to his
father's early home to pass the hot
weather, and spent most of the next
three months out of the city accompa-
nied by his mother and Esau, who had
become so accustomed to wait upon him
as to be almost indispensable.

" One of the dearest recollections I
have of Rossie," says a valued friend, " is
that on a brilliant summer afternoon,

when, after a long and pleasant drive together, we stopped at a beautiful place,
where a friend was staying, and went
wandering down garden pathways and
through a great greenhouse and grap-
ery.

"There was nothing that escaped Rossie's eye, — no tint of leaf, or flower, or
fruit, no effect of sun or shadow; but
after a little while, becoming weary, he
slipped his slender hand over my arm,
and went with me toward a cool and
shady retreat in the lower part of the
garden. On his way he looked up at
me with those bright, wistful eyes of his,
and asked, "When did you and I begin
to be friends?" I have forgotten my
exact answer, but from this, I remember
how he went on talking of his likings for
persons. This talk was not light and un-

thinking chatter; it was thoughtful and full of his peculiar wisdom; it showed plainly that his likings were founded on real insight into character.

But, with all this delicacy of insight, this unusual maturity of mind, he had, too, the genuine love of fun and frolic and what boyish pursuits it was possible for him to follow.

And this love of fun, together with his quickness of perception, often led him to make remarks that were long remembered for their wit. For instance, in the first of the war, when there was so much talk of what should be done with the traitor Jeff. Davis, when he was caught, and one was prophesying one thing, and another another, all agreeing that some terrible punishment must befall him, Rossie, listening one day to this talk,

remarked, "Hum! they wont do anything with him but put him in a feather-
bed." The curiously clear conception of
the leniency with which the traitor would
be treated in the event of his capture —
a conception which seems like something prophetic now — is an instance of
the peculiarity of his mind. Those who
knew him well could go on telling story
after story of this kind, and of his
goodness, too, his piety and trust in God
and in that heaven, which to him only
appeared another home, where his life
would go on painless and freed from all
the weariness which this contained for
him. To that home he has now attained;
there he walks truly a freed spirit, no
longer cramped by the fetters of the
flesh, the suffering little body. We
can no longer say from our pity, " Poor

little Rossie!" for he is now rich, — rich in the kingdom of heaven.

When the summer was over, he was glad to go back again to his home. The curvature of his spine had increased, and he was unable to move about without crutches, and grew constantly weaker and more full of pain, which he bore with the utmost bravery.

He did not return to the room in which he had passed the last winter, but took a small one, opening into a larger, in which he slept. In the little one were arranged his curiosities, working materials, etc., but we will let him describe it for himself in a letter to a comparative stranger, dated, —

"PROVIDENCE, Oct., 1866.

" *My Dear Friend,* — I was very much pleased when I received the two papers, to find that you still remembered me. I have thought often of you since the day of my trip to Rocky Point, and I shall never forget your kindness there, and I have wondered a great deal if ever I should hear from you or see you again; and it gives me great pleasure to know that I am still remembered, and I flatter myself so much as to think that you would like to have me write to you, for it will be a satisfaction to myself to thank you again for your kind attentions.

"I have had two very severe attacks since I saw you. That day was a very trying day for me; I did too much, and so, as soon as I got home, I had to give up entirely. Still, I cannot say that I regret it; I am willing to suffer considerably for the sake of enjoying so much.

I do not know as I shall ever go again,
for if I walk now over a rod at a time, I
have a return of the pain. I suppose it is
neuralgia.

" The papers came while I was in bed,
and I read them with much interest.
They proved a great comfort to me, and
amused me for a long time, and helped
me to forget my pains. I did not see
a great deal of your little daughter.
How I wish I could see you both in my
little sitting-room! I think in a very
little while we should know each other.
It is a difficult thing to get acquainted in
such a crowd as thronged past us every
moment.

" My room is about ten feet square.
All my things are here, — my museum,
my sewing materials, books, etc. I write
a great deal, — I love to, — and nothing

would please me more than to have you for a correspondent. I love to hear from my friends, now and then, — the oftener the better. I enjoy myself very much though I am sick; I have every-thing to make me happy, besides every luxury that kind parents can procure; I have those comforts which many well people have not, — the comforts of reli-gion. If it were not for these, I could not live and be happy.

"I hope you will think this letter worth answering. Remember me to your little girl, and believe me to be your very affectionate little excursionist,

"Roswell Park Perry."

A physician who frequently visited the family says of him, "Rossie had the impatient and suffering temperament, and the great wonder is that he manifested so much patience under such severe and protracted pain. He suffered from awful attacks of neuralgia which he once told me would 'come as sudden as lightning and drive the screeches out of him.'"

One of Rossie's great comforts was listening to reading, and he was always interested in such books as his mother and older friends would naturally choose for themselves. History and "Littell's Living Age" had long shared his attention, and "Our Young Folks," with its riddles and rebuses; but the Bible had always a fresh charm for him, and of that alone he never wearied. He delighted in poetry, particularly hymns, which, though he was not strong enough to recite himself, he often asked his friends to repeat for him. One which interested him very much at this time, from its touching description of his own position, was this : —

" I am kneeling at the threshold, weary, faint, and sore,
Waiting for the dawning, for the opening of the door, —
Waiting till the Master shall bid me rise and come
To the glory of his presence, to the gladness of his home.

" A weary path I've travelled, 'mid darkness, storm, and
strife,
Bearing many a burden, struggling for my life ,
But now the morn is breaking ; my toil will soon be o'er ;
I'm kneeling at the threshold, my hand is on the door !

" Methinks I hear the voices of the blessed, as they stand
Singing in the sunshine, in the far-off, sinless land :
Oh ! would that I were with them, amid their shining
throng,
Mingling in their worship, joining in their song !

" With them the blessed angels, that know no grief or sin ;
I see them by the portals, prepared to let me in.
O Lord, I wait thy pleasure ; thy time and way are
best ;
But I'm wasted, worn, and weary ; O Father, bid me
rest ! "

IX.

NEARING THE BEAUTIFUL CITY.

"O mother dear, Jerusalem !
When shall I come to thee ?
When shall my sorrows have an end ?
Thy joys when shall I see ? "

THE last winter of Rossie's life was one of very great interest to the friends who clustered about him. His room, which had been the cheerful rendezvous of the boys, was so no longer; he was not able to receive long calls from them, but he welcomed them cheerfully, as they came in to talk with him for a moment, and loved to think that they did not forget him. White and Esau were sometimes taught there, and though Rossie's failing strength would not allow him to instruct them himself, his interest and care for them never flagged. The little wasted invalid, who could not move, nor even be touched, without pain, would, as long as he was able, try to teach them to repeat Bible verses from his beloved scroll. Esau had learned to repeat correctly the first part of the fourteenth chapter of St. John, and frequently recited it to soothe the restless hours of his little master.

Numberless little errands, necessary for the work, which he still kept up, were readily performed by the members of the family, always rewarded by the grateful look and never-failing, "Thank you," that acknowledged every service, however slight. He had expressed a wish that, if it were God's will, he might live till after Christmas; for, though so feeble, he had prepared, with his own hands, some little gift for each one of his family friends, and he wished to present those gifts himself. Seated in one side of his little rocking-chair, with his feet drawn up under him, always supporting his head with one hand, unless it were propped up with pillows, he might be seen engaged in drawing very nice pictures for his mother; then, seeking relief in a change of employment, he would embroider the initials of some loved one on a handkerchief, or work on a dressing-case, which, with the aid of his mother, he was preparing for another. He showed great judgment in the selection of his gifts, and his friends were often surprised to find their wants anticipated, by the dear boy's thoughtful love.

On Christmas-day, he dined with the family for the last time, the excitement of the occasion, the giving and receiving of gifts, the unusual stir around him, so fatigued him, that he was glad to be taken back to the quiet of his own room, early in the afternoon; and he left that room but once again, until he passed to the mansion prepared for him above.

Among his many beautiful presents, Rossie particularly enjoyed an illuminated text, "Look unto me, and be ye saved," which was at once added to the many ornaments of his room, and delighted his eyes and his heart so long as earthly joys could reach them.

A few Sundays before his last, at his own request, the communion was administered to him. Two or three besides the family were present, and it was an occasion of deepest interest to all; but to little Rossie it was very joyful; the night after his heart was so full of joy that he could not sleep, but at midnight was heard singing, —

> " I'm going home, I'm going home,
> I'm going home to die no more."

" Oh, how happy I am," he said. " What makes me so happy ? " He was told that it must be because Jesus was near him, and he replied, " Yes, I feel just as I did when I first gave him my heart," adding, " If I do live, I shall ask Dr. Swain to come again and administer the communion ; wouldn't it be proper ? "

On New Year's day, he asked for a new diary, having been accustomed, for two or three years, to note anything of interest in one. When it was brought, him, he wrote the record of the day, then turned to the 5th of April, and wrote,

9

"This is my birthday; I am fifteen years old," then pointing to the words with a cheerful smile, he observed, "I've written it, auntie, but do you think I'll be here then?"

About this time, Rossie said that he wished each of his friends to have some reminder of him, and he would like to arrange for this himself; so he wanted to make his will. This document he asked his aunt to write out for him, thinking that the idea would pain his mother. He left to his father a favorite bust of General Grant; to his mother, a beautiful watch-chain, which he had purchased with his own money; to his brother, the desk which had been so close a companion to him; to his aunt, the silver fork, marked with his name, with which he had always eaten. The many beautiful books and presents, which had been given him, he divided among relatives and friends, remembering each one with some special sign of constant love, not forgetting to leave to White and Esau some substantial proofs of his thoughtful care for them.

Rossie quietly planned about his funeral, mentioned the clothing in which he wanted his body dressed for the grave, asked that his friends would sit around it during the last ceremonies, and particularly requested that it might be buried in some cheerful, pretty place, which would be pleasant for his parents to visit. His wishes were obeyed, and the worn body lies at Swan Point, a beautiful cemetery in the neighborhood of Providence.

He often asked to hear his favorite hymns, especially this one : —

My God, whose gracious pity I may claim,
 Calling thee Father, — sweet, endearing name !
The sufferings of this weak and weary frame, —
  All, all are known to thee.

From human eye, 'tis better to conceal
 Much that I suffer, much I hourly feel;
But oh ! the thought does tranquillize and heal, —
  All, all is known to thee.

Each secret conflict with indwelling sin,
 Each sickening fear, I ne'er the prize shall win,
Each pang from irritation, turmoil, din, —
  All, all are known to thee.

When in the morning unrefreshed I wake,
 Or in the night but little sleep can take,
This brief appeal submissively I make, —
  All, all is known to thee.

Nay, all by thee is ordered, chosen, planned, —
 Each drop that fills my daily cup ; thy hand
Prescribes for ills none else can understand, —
  All, all is known to thee.

The effectual means to cure what I deplore ;
 In me thy longed-for likeness to restore ;
Self to dethrone, never to govern more, —
  All, all are known to thee.

And this continued feebleness, this state,
 Which seems to unnerve and incapacitate,

Will work the cure, my hopes and prayers await, —
  That can I leave to thee.

Nor will the bitter draught distasteful prove,
  When I recall the Son of thy dear love;
The cup thou wouldst not, for *our* sakes remove,
  That cup *he* drank for *me*.

And welcome, precious, can his Spirit make
  My little drop of suffering for his sake;
Father, the cup I drink, the path I take, —
  All, all is known to thee.

Which, he said, expressed just what *his* heart said to his heavenly Father.

As Rossie's death approached, he could not even be touched without pain. During the daily trial of getting him up, a friend said to him, "Poor little fellow, what a glorious change it will be for you to be where you can move about, as you choose, and will not have to think of this poor suffering little body!"

He looked at her with a bright smile, and said, "Oh, wont it!" as if the pros-

pect afforded him unspeakable satisfaction. The last Saturday of his life he
seemed a little better and his father,
who was feeling his pulse, said to him,
" Rossie, you are better; I shouldn't wonder if you lived a month."

" A month, father!" was the reply in a
dejected tone, — " a month more of this!"

When his father went out, he said, in
real distress, " How can I stay here
another month! What object is there in
it? I've finished all my work; what can
I do?"

He was told that if God spared his life,
he would find something for him to do,
and would be sure to take care of him, if
he kept him longer on the earth, when
he said, reflectively, " Then I cannot be
thinking of it all the time."

His friend said to him that he would

better not try, and that she should not care whether God's messenger found her about some household labor, or engaged in prayer, if she were doing his will.

" Well, then," said he, "I mean to act as if I were to live till the millennium."

So the next time he saw his father, he said, "Father, I want to take a sleigh-ride."

The roads and the weather were bad, and he had been thought too feeble even to be taken down-stairs for a long time, but his father promised him a sleigh-ride on Monday, if he then wished to go. Accordingly, on that day he took a short ride in a large covered sleigh, his father and mother holding him in their arms, so that he felt no motion, and he returned much delighted with his drive. His whole appearance was so deathlike that

a dear friend, who had called just before
he went out, feared he would never come
back alive, and remained at the house
until his return, when he talked cheerfully to her, describing what he had seen
in his ride. The next day, he sent for
White and Esau, wishing that they
should be told how very sick he was, and
that he could probably never hear them
read again. They came for the last time,
White bringing his Testament, and Esau
receiving one from his young master.
They read the parable of the Prodigal
Son, and the twenty-third Psalm. Rossie listened with attention, occasionally
making a remark, or correcting a mistake, but was so thoroughly wearied, when
they had finished, that he could not talk
to them, as he had wished, but was obliged
to delegate to another the task of ex-

pressing "all that I wanted to say to them."

A letter from an intimate friend speaks of him so truly and touchingly, that we will not apologize for inserting it here.

"One who most sincerely loved our sainted Rossie, and who feels that the confidence and love expressed by him to her are among her choicest remembrances, wishes to add her tribute to his memory. The story of this short life, so crowded with suffering, and yet fulfilling so holy a mission, must be a comfort to many children, who, like him, are debarred from childish sports, and the free motion of their limbs, showing them how much may be enjoyed, and how much good may be done by a Christian child, even while suffering most intense bodily pain.

"I can see Rossie now, propped in his easy-chair, his chin resting in his hand, and though suffering much, interesting himself in every subject of conversation that came up, and furnishing more original ideas than any of his older listeners, saying such quaint and witty things that one wondered how old a soul inhabited that poor little body.

"Rossie was scarcely ever idle, and many a result of his industry and taste remain as reminders of how patiently he labored towards any end he had in view.

"He was a true friend, and the spirit with which he defended those he loved in their absence is something we seldom see in one of his years. If he could not

understand the motive in anything his
friends said or did, he would be sure to
get them to explain it to him, instead of
remarking upon it to others. He was
always cordial, and ready to share all his
delicacies with those who came to see
him.

"I shall never forget a conversation I
had with him on a ride one day, about
that dear brother whom he was permitted so soon to meet in heaven. He
spoke of the different points in his
brother's experience, in a way which
showed that he saw clearly the requisites
of the Christian life, and yet so simple
and direct that no one could doubt his
having been taught of Jesus. Rossie had
no *cant* about him; indeed, nothing distressed him more than those unnatural

expressions of so-called piety, which we often hear.

"As his sufferings increased, he looked forward to his rest, 'with joy and not with grief.' He scarcely ever alluded to that part of death which naturally appalls us, but seemed most mercifully to have been permitted always to see 'beyond the river.' He knew in whom he had trusted, and he was not afraid.

"He said to me the week before he died, 'I've had a great disappointment to-day. You see I have flattered myself with the idea that I should soon be at rest; in the morning I would think I should go before night, and at night before the morning; but here I linger, linger, linger. I asked my father to-day how long he thought I could live, and he said, "Rossie, you may live a month;"

but you've no idea, how my heart sank within me, as he said this.' Now that he has reached his heavenly home, can we not hear him, in imagination, singing to his harp of gold, —

'No sin, no grief, no pain,
  Safe in my happy home,
My fears all fled, my doubts all slain,
  My hour of triumph come!
Ah! friends of my mortal years,
  The trusted and the true,
You are walking still in that vale of tears,
  But I wait to welcome you.' "

X.

THE BEAUTIFUL CITY.

"Which when I had seen, I wished myself among them."

THE terror of death had never had power over Rossie; singularly brave in the endurance of physical pain, and fearless by natural temperament, his loving, longing eagerness to meet his Saviour would allow no fear. "There'll be no dark valley for me," he said; "there was none for Mrs. Swain, you know," — alluding to the wife of his minister, who had lately died most happily. "I shall go right over the river to see Jesus."

But, though there was no darkness, the way was long; through many hours of a long, heavy snow-storm, the parting soul tarried on the threshold of perfect life; the stricken group around him murmured, " He is going, going," but the response of the ministering angels (we almost heard it) was, " Coming, coming."

While his friends thought him dying, he was trying to calm his father, saying, " Oh, father, don't, dear father, don't cry! I'm so happy now." His breathing was like that of the dying, and he asked, " How long can this last ? " Then, as his father touched the pulse, " How long can it beat ? "

" About half an hour," was the re-ply, " Then you don't think I'll be dis-appointed this time ; do you ? "

" No, Rossie, I think you are certainly dying."

He wished for prayer, and when asked

"For what shall I pray?" answered, "Lord Jesus, come quickly."

After a short prayer, he gave some final charges, — to his father, "to meet him in heaven," to his brother, "to be a consistent Christian," something to every member of the family; and then said, "Tell Esau he must be a Christian," and, "Tell everybody that I love them."

With the old longing to be remembered, he asked where a lately painted picture of himself would be placed. His mother said, "I suppose you would like to have it hung where we can all see it."

"Yes," said he, "for I shall always be behind it, or," — correcting himself, — "beside it."

He then said, "Mother, you have no likeness of my little brother," — a babe who had died before Rossie's birth. " How shall I know him ?"

" He will come and meet you," was his mother's reply.

" And I will come and meet you when any of you come to heaven."

Contrary to all expectations, he was somewhat relieved by restoratives, and fell asleep, and when he woke, his enunciation, till then clear and strong, was very imperfect, and he was obliged to express himself mostly by gestures. In this way, he lingered all through the next day, sleeping a little, and rousing occasionally, but perfectly calm. In the night, he asked, by signs, for pencil and paper, and a book, on which to write, and a little Sunday-school singing-book was handed to him. He immediately turned to the hymn, " We are waiting by the river," and asked to have it read, then attempted to sing it, but was unable. Afterwards he commenced writing, " To all whom I know." His sight was failing, and he asked if this could be read; then he took up his pencil for another effort, but merely wrote, " Oh, I'm too sleepy," and laid it aside forever. Before the dawn he begged to have his parents called, and wanted them to sing, " We are waiting by the river," then fell into a heavy sleep.

A few moments before he died, his father came into his chamber; he held out his little hand to him, and said, in very tender tones, " I'm here, papa." The strong, loving arms lifted him into an easier position. Just then the sun broke through the heavy clouds of that long, dreary storm and filled the room with

golden light, and the long storm of afflic-
tions that one little sufferer had endured
so patiently was over forever : the sun
of an Eternal Life arose for him, and
without a struggle, he passed into the
glory beyond the veil.

Now we sing his song, —

> We are waiting by the river,
>   We are watching on the shore,
> Only waiting for the boatman,
>   Soon he'll come to bear us o'er.
>
> Though the mist hang o'er the river,
>   And its billows loudly roar,
> Yet we hear the song of angels
>   Wafted on the other shore.
>
> And the bright celestial city,
>   We have caught most radiant gleams
> Of its towers like dazzling sunlight,
>   With its sweet and peaceful streams,
>
> He has called for many a loved one ;
>   We have seen them leave our side ;
> With our Saviour we shall meet them
>   When we too have crossed the tide.

When we've passed that vale of shadows,
　With its dark and chilling tide,
In that bright and glorious City
　We shall evermore abide.

Chorus.

We are waiting by the river,
　We are watching on the shore,
Only waiting for the boatman,
　Soon he'll come to bear us o'er.

XI.

REUNION.

"We pass from the clasp of mourning friends
To the arms of the loved and lost,
And those smiling faces will greet us there,
Which on earth we have valued most."

E have followed our little Rossie's life — that life of so few years, and so much trial and development — as far as mortal eyes can see its progress; now we turn to cast one glance at another life, that, moving from the same point, through a very different path, reached the goal only a little later. The darling brother, who gave so much comfort and joy to the wasted invalid, formed a thorough contrast to him in personal ap-

pearance. Grosvenor was in perfect
health, tall and strong, with light hair
and bright blue eyes, and had the powerful magnetism of young, earnest life
about him. He was gentle, and "easy
to be entreated," singularly simple and
truthful in nature, — one whom all loved
and respected, for unaffected beauty
of character and genuine manliness. It
was a lesson to many of his elders to
see the untiring patience, with which he
cared for his poor brother, using his
own health and strength to serve every
caprice of sickness, and always ready to
yield his plans to brighten that shad-
owed life. He was nearly four years
older than Rossie, and when his parents
stood by the grave of their youngest,
they could feel that earth had yet much
for them, as they looked at their noble

son, who had begun to develop the
manliness of his fine nature, according to
" the power of an endless life," and stood
before them ready for vigorous, useful
work in the world. Grosvenor had chosen
his father's profession, and was preparing
to bring his eager enthusiasm to the aid
of mature experience, when accident suddenly checked his bounding health.

As he was playing *base-ball*, in which
he excelled, and at the time of the Uni-
versity match between the students of
Harvard and Brown, he strained his side
severely, and was obliged to leave the
game and go home at once. No one
thought of danger, but it was there; perhaps the sufferer himself felt, more than
others, that he was badly hurt; but his
repeated question, " Is my life in danger ? "
was answered with repeated assurances

that it was not, and he resigned himself quietly to the few days of inaction which would recruit the strained muscles, and enable him to return again to his busy student life. After about a fortnight of this enforced quiet, with no very great suffering, an unexpected change alarmed his physicians, and he was told that he could live but a short time. He was rapidly growing weaker, and could say but little; but that little expressed a calm acquiescence in the divine will which cut off the strong hopes that had leaped forward to life's activities, and a firm confidence in the Lord who doeth all things well. In ten hours from the announcement of his danger, he died gently and easily; and the two brothers, separated but for six months, were united again forever.

Their lives had passed through different channels: one had taken a rough course, where many rocks lay in the way and it was hard to pass; one had always run smoothly, till that final plunge into the great ocean of eternity; but both reached alike happily and trustingly the same goal.

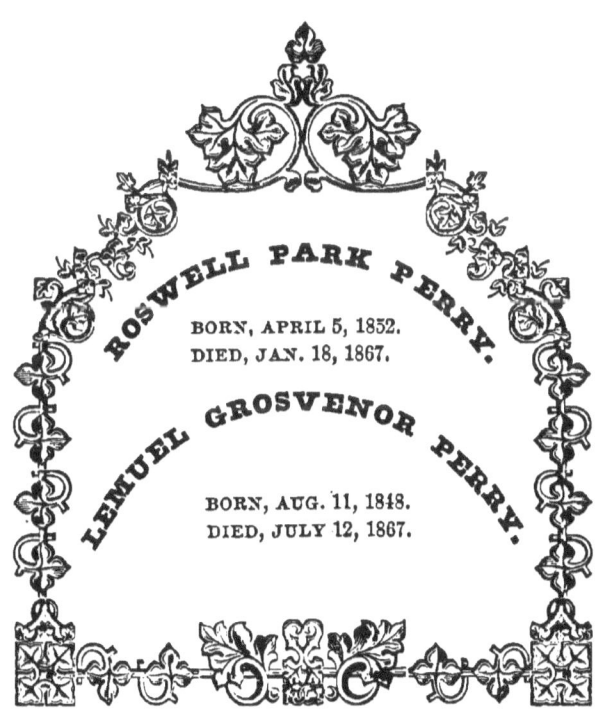

ROSWELL PARK PERRY.

BORN, APRIL 5, 1852.
DIED, JAN. 18, 1867.

LEMUEL GROSVENOR PERRY.

BORN, AUG. 11, 1848.
DIED, JULY 12, 1867.

THE THREE SONS.

I HAVE a son, a little son,
  A boy just five years old,
With eyes of thoughtful earnestness
  And mind of gentle mould:
They tell me that unusual grace
  In all his ways appears,
That my child is wise and grave of heart
  Beyond his childish years.
I cannot say how this may be;
  I know his face is fair,
And yet his chiefest comeliness
  Is his sweet and serious air;
I know his heart is kind and fond,
  I know he loveth me,
But loveth yet his mother more,
  With grateful fervency.
But that which others most admire
  Is the thought that fills his mind,
The food for grave, inquiring speech
  He everywhere doth find.
Strange questions doth he ask of me,

When we together walk;
He scarcely thinks as children think,
 Or talks as children talk :
Nor cares he much for childish sports,
 Dotes not on bat or ball,
But looks on manhood's ways and works,
 And aptly mimics all.
His little heart is busy still,
 And oftentimes perplexed
With thoughts about this world of ours,
 And thoughts about the next.
He kneels at his dear mother's knee,
 She teacheth him to pray,
And strange and sweet and solemn then
 Are the words which he will say.
Oh ! should my gentle child be spared
 To manhood's years, like me,
A holier and a wiser man,
 I trust that he will be ;
But when I look into his eyes,
 And on his thoughtful brow,
I dare not think what I should feel,
 If I should lose him now.

I have a son, a second son,
 A simple child of three.
I'll not declare, how bright and fair
 His little features be :
How silver sweet those tones of his,

When he prattles on my knee:
I do not think his bright blue eye
   Is like his brother's keen,
Nor his brow so full of childish thought,
   As his has ever been;
But his little heart's a fountain pure
   Of kind and tender feeling,
And his every look a gleam of light,
   Rich depths of love revealing:
When he walks with me, the country folks,
   Who pass us in the street,
Will shout for joy, and bless my boy,
   He looks so mild and sweet.
A playfellow is he to all,
   And yet with cheerful tone,
Will sing his little song of love,
   When left to sport alone.
His presence is like sunshine, sent
   To gladden home and hearth,
To comfort us in all our griefs,
   And sweeten all our mirth.
Should he grow up to riper years,
   God grant his heart may prove
As sweet a home for heavenly grace
   As now for earthly love;
And if, beside his grave, the tears
   Our aching eyes must dim,
God comfort us for all the love
   That we shall lose in him.

I have a son, a third sweet son;
  His age I cannot tell,
For they reckon not by years and months
  Where he has gone to dwell.
To us, for fourteen anxious months,
  His infant smiles were given,
And then he bade farewell to earth,
  And went to live in heaven.
I cannot tell what form is his,
  What look he weareth now,
Nor guess how bright a glory crowns
  His shining seraph brow;
But I know, for God hath told me this,
  That he is now at rest,
Where other blessed infants be,
  On the Saviour's loving breast.
Whate'er befalls his brethren twain,
  His bliss can never cease;
Their lot may here be grief and pain,
  But his is certain peace.
It may be that the tempter's wiles,
  Their souls from bliss may sever,
But, if our own poor faith fail not,
  He must be ours forever.
When we think of what our darling is
  And what we still must be;
When we muse on that world's perfect bliss,
  And this world's misery;

When we groan beneath this load of sin,
   And feel this grief and pain, —
Oh! we'd rather lose our other two
   Than have him here again.

                    REV. JOHN MOULTRIE.

The End.